HIP, HOP, HOORAY
FOR
BROOKLYNN BUNNY!

JILL HAROLD AND BETSY MILLER

Thinking Ink Press
Campbell, California

This book is dedicated to my precious
Brooklynn Kristine Harold,
who amazes me every day with her love.
—Jill Harold

For Cristina and Takeshi.
—Betsy Miller

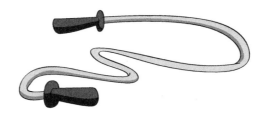

When Brooklynn Bunny was a baby, she had bright eyes, silky ears, and a strong kick.

Brooklynn's family noticed that her paws were twisted. "How will she hop?" said Bryson.

"We love hopping!" said Brayden. "Every summer we have so much fun at the Hippity Hop Games!"

4

Brooklynn's ears perked up. She couldn't wait to get big enough to hop.

"Brooklynn, don't worry about a thing," said Mama Bunny.

"We will get your paws straight, and you'll be hopping all over the place!" said Papa Bunny.

"Hop, hop, hop!" said Brooklynn.

The Bunny family hopped over to see Dr. Bear. Dr. Bear gently stretched and turned Brooklynn's paws and put on casts. Brooklynn visited Dr. Bear many times and had a small surgery. When the last casts came off, Brooklynn's paws were straight.

"Hip, hop, hooray!" cheered the Bunny family.

"Now it's time for you to visit Mr. Boots to get a pair of super boots to keep your paws straight," said Dr. Bear.

"What are super boots?" asked Mama Bunny.

"Special boots to wear at nighttime," said Dr. Bear.

"Hello, Brooklynn," said Mr. Boots. "What color super boots would you like?"

Brooklynn wiggled her bunny nose with excitement. "Pink!" she said.

"Brooklynn is going to wear boots in bed!" said Bryson.
"No shoes or boots on the furniture!" said Brayden.
"Super boots are a special case," said Papa Bunny.

Mr. Boots measured Brooklynn's paws. Her super boots fit just right.

"The heels and toes are open so they are more comfortable to sleep in," said Mr. Boots. He smiled and tickled Brooklynn's toes. "Brooklynn, you need to wear your super boots every night to keep your paws straight so that you can hop all day. Do you promise?"

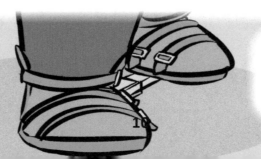

"I promise," said Brooklynn.

Brooklynn wore her super boots every night.

Before long, she was hopping with her brothers in the daytime. They played hopscotch and hide-and-seek. But Brooklynn wanted to learn to hop rope most of all.

The first time Brooklynn tried hop rope, the rope got tangled in her ears.

Brooklynn did not give up. She tried and tried until she could hop rope one time.

Brooklynn made up a hop rope rhyme. "Hop, and stop! Hop, and stop!"

The rhyme helped Brooklynn to get better at hop rope. She hopped twice in a row and ran inside to tell Mama Bunny.

"That's wonderful!" said Mama Bunny. "I was just signing up Bryson and Brayden for the sack race at the Hippity Hop Games."

15

"Can you sign me up for hop rope?" said Brooklynn.
"The rules say you have to be able to hop at least ten times in a row. Can you do that?" said Mama Bunny.

"Not yet, but I will keep trying."
"OK," said Mama Bunny. "I will sign you up and write a note that you are trying to learn."

"Yay for Brooklynn!" said Bryson and Brayden.
"Hip, hop, hooray!" said Brooklynn.

Brooklynn hopped in the garden. "Hippity hopping, never stopping! Hippity hopping, never stopping!"

She hopped at the park.

"Hop to the left!

Hop to the right!"

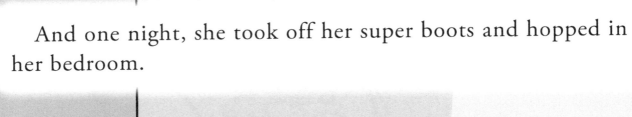

And one night, she took off her super boots and hopped in her bedroom.

"Hop all day and hop all night!"

20

The Bunny family came in to see what the noise was. "Brooklynn," said Mama Bunny, "it's time for bed. Let's get your super boots back on and tuck you in."

"No!" said Brooklynn. "I want to keep hopping!"

"We're proud of you for practicing," said Papa Bunny. "But wearing your super boots is important to keep your paws straight so that you can hop. Remember, you promised to wear your super boots every night."

"You can hop rope tomorrow," said Mama Bunny.

"OK," said Brooklynn. "Just one more hop before bed.
I wear my super boots every night
So I can hop with all my might!"

The next night, the Bunnys heard a racket coming from Brooklynn's room and went to see what it was.

"We're proud of you for practicing hop rope," said Mama Bunny.

"And we're proud of you for wearing your super boots," said Papa Bunny.

"But not at the same time!" they said together.

Soon it was time for the Hippity Hop Games.

Bryson and Brayden had a great time in the sack race while Brooklynn cheered them on.

Then it was time for hop rope. Brooklynn took a deep breath and started hopping.

"Hippity hopping, never stopping!
Hippity hopping, never stopping!

"Hop to the left,

Hop to the right,

Hop all day and that's all right!

I wear my super boots every night
So I can hop with all my might!

29

"Wow!" said Brooklynn. "I hopped 32 times!"
The Bunnys cheered, "Hip, hop, hooray for Brooklynn!"

THE END

Dear reader,

Brooklynn Bunny and her family are based on a real girl named Brooklynn and her family. The real Brooklynn likes to play in the daytime, and she wears super boots at nighttime, just like Brooklynn Bunny. We were so excited when Brooklynn joined our family, and we're happy to share this story with you.

Keep trying and you can accomplish anything!

Sincerely,
Josh, Jill, Bryson, Brayden, and Brooklynn Harold

P.S. You can connect with Brooklynn Bunny online:
Website: www.BrooklynnBunny.com
Facebook: www.facebook.com/BrooklynnBunny
Twitter: @BrooklynnBunny

FOR PARENTS OF CHILDREN WHO WEAR A BRACE

Congratulations on having a wonderful child! Brooklynn exceeded our every expectation with how much happiness and perseverance comes with a child born with clubfoot. This journey requires an incredible amount of dedication and commitment. Continue to stay persistent. Your child is perfect.

Here are some tips to make your journey as smooth as possible and to prepare you to make informed decisions for your child:

- Learn about proper treatment for your child, and don't be afraid to ask questions.
- Talk honestly with your child and siblings if they have questions about your child's treatment.
- Have a support system. You may want to connect with other families in the same situation.
- Locate a skilled doctor.
- Remember that there is more to your child than treatment. Have fun with your child and enjoy your time together.

ABOUT THE AUTHORS

Jill Harold created the online support group Clubfoot Community of California and manages the Clubfoot Shoe Exchange USA and Clubfoot Journey groups. She became involved with clubfoot support groups when her daughter was born with clubfoot, and she was inspired to write this book to help other families on a similar journey. Jill (Mama Bunny) is an elementary school teacher who lives in California with her husband Josh (Papa Bunny) and three little children bunnies: Bryson, Brayden, and Brooklynn.

Betsy Miller is the author of the children's stories "Straight, Strong, and Stretchy" and "The Piñata Moon" as well as the nonfiction books *The Parents' Guide to Clubfoot*, *The Parents' Guide to Perthes*, and *The Parents' Guide to Hip Dysplasia*. She teamed up with Jill Harold to write *Hip, Hop, Hooray for Brooklynn Bunny* to share what a little fun and a lot of persistence can lead to in life. Betsy loved to jump rope with her friends when she was growing up, and she had fun making up the jump rope rhymes for this book.

CPSIA information can be obtained
at www.ICGtesting.com
Printed in the USA
LVOW05s0330290317
528836LV00027B/646/P